Congratulations ! !
hold in your hand a
collection of poetry & prose
by the great-great-great-
great grandson of Jean

THE ART OF MUTINY

by

Baptiste

Fletcher Christian Redux

Trotochaud.

The man who donated
the land for the St. Francis
Solanus Indian Mission Church,
Petoskey, Michigan.
Yours in Christ !
FCR

"Meticulously researched. Yet the question remains: what was he researching?"
        –Ebb Tide, *Charybdis Chronicle*

"You'll laugh, cry, and foam at the mouth. In summary, you'll shamelessly emote. Read only in a safe space!"
        – Limited Asymptote

"Parody or satire? Of itself, maybe."
        – @gooselakeacidtrip

"*Naked Lunch* for the square world."
        – Gantt C. Hart, *OnSchedule*

"With creeping trepidation that modernity's *de facto* penalty for exercising one's 5th Amendment right is [REDACTED], I, nonetheless, on counsel's advice, neither confirm nor deny the veracity of this *composition most foul.*"
        – @montresorsrevenge

"Manic Genius/Depressive Brilliance. Honestly, unmercifully, and utterly true to form, F.C. Redux either kills himself or dies trying."
        – Chester Fangs, *Paté Post*

DEDICATED

To those who won't ask if it's for them.

INVOCATION

Not sacred scripture.
Nor even wise counsel.
Scarcely even a single objective,
indisputable
fact.

For, who?
is the writer
but
a compiler of oral histories,
a chronicler of inner monologues,
an interpreter of dreams?

Do falcons fear gravity?
Do anglerfish crave sunshine and
fresh air?
Do winds brake before canyon walls?

LAST NIGHT

oh, subconscious spectre
fire for effect your
cadaverous cannon

ming vase monstrosity
shattered glass
explosion
my gripping, paralyzing
broken glass
phobia

mortuary tones

you're the shaman
now
you're the brujo
now

spirit worlds
speak
through dreams

see you tomorrow
night

WYLDE'S WEST

Packard diesels spin
decrepit shafts
seething frustration

As you gaze upon
horizon spearing
snow-capped peaks

"Damn this boat."
"What's that you say?"
"I said damn this boat."

Dock and tie and run
Map and keys and can I see your ID?

"Whatever."
"What's that you say?"
"Nothing, I just want to get going."

Portland recedes
Mount Hood fills
Your Soul's Vision

Today you breathe

Deep,
Sweet
Cascadia Air

PUNCHLINE

freedom
is realizing what you have
is what no one wants
because people want stuff
not
freedom

NOWHERE MAN

TODAY

Theme Park drill.

Back and forth and forth and back in
snaking roped off lines.

Bored. Then board.

The Ride – a single minute's panic-
exhilaration.

You screech-halt and dismount on
the nightmare's dark side.

What she said
about "date night."

But we're not talking about that here.

We're talking airport security.
And you made it through. Again.
It's 623am so you put your laptop
back in its case and your belt back
through its loops and your shoes
back on your feet and wonder why
you didn't renew PRECHECK and
wouldn't it be nice to fly private
again or better yet drive but despite
the relative unimportance of this job
and minimal time-sensitivity, driving
a car (even yours) to Turks and
Caicos is out of the question, boats
are too slow (even for this) and The
Syndicate long ago sold off its fixed-
wing assets..

So, you get in line for a spot of over-
roasted, burnt SBC (Seattle's Big
Corporate) coffee. While your mind,
ritually, habitually, wanders to what
it is you're doing here and why.

YESTERDAY

Per routine, it started far beyond
early.

A particularly patterned knock at the
door. You might describe it as "bu da
wa da, bu da," but that's inarticulate.

9

Not to mention wrong.

No, this knock's sophisticated.

It's that old Watt-sy jazz meshed with
Bonham brutality.

Bill Ward's restrained "Junior's
Eyes" punishments?

Or Jimmy Chamberlin's pummeling
"Muzzle"?

No, it's surely Sabbath – off either
Ecstasy or *Die!*

Legend has it Ozzy thought the boys
had gone poofter but, in hindsight,
can't we all agree that by providing
an obvious bridge to the NWOBHM,
the final two founding-quartet
Sabbath albums are, in fact,
historically significant and, indeed,
FAR from lacking in artistic merit?

And foggy though YOUR head may
be, Black Dog snaps into total recall,
lets out a ripper of a growl-yelp-bark
and sprints for the entryway.

Five separate deadbolt-turns later, you open the door (outward because hurricanes) and feast your eyes upon...

The Syndicate's eternal artistry on display – again.

Recognition's brief flash. Bhutan or Burma? Lower latitude, sea-level majority-Buddhist principalities?

Reality beckons.

Mentally noting to increase your B^{12} regimen, you consciously move on while your subconscious toils away.

"Ready?" she purrs.
"If you say" you mumble.
"I say."

"Time for a cocktail?"
"At 4am?"

"It's only early if you've been to bed. And I haven't."

"Well, I have."

[You wonder with whom and where and for what time did she set her alarm?]

Half-heartedly you inquire, "Gear?"

"Just you. Unless, of course, you didn't check your mail yesterday. In that case we'll have to swing by your P.O. box."

"Nah, I got 'em. Even turned 'em on." [Knowing full well you didn't.]

"I know full well you didn't."

"Right then. Well, I trust you're driving so we'll do it in the car."

"Here's an idea, Eff-See: how about for once you surprise us by not being such a low-return slipknot reactionary?"

"My Caymans account speaks to a higher valuation."

"Because you're so far lower left you loop around into upper right. As if we multiplied two negative numbers then squared the result, ending up

12

with a positive, an order of magnitude beyond what's forecasted from the raw materials."

"You really should try my cocktails next time."

"There won't be one."

"A next time or a cocktail?"

"You do realize The Syndicate's updated handler training module inoculated me against your less-than charming persistence."

"They need to trash that whole program. Start over from scratch. And tell them in the future to please send a rookie – one naïve enough to be wowed by my charm, looks, mixology skills, musical taste, handsome, yet exuberantly goofy (or goofily exuberant?) rescue Pitador and small arms collection. Not some worn-out, jaded, teetotaling over-achiever with zero appreciation for what is good in life."

"I am not a teetotaler. Or worn-out."
"Prove it."

And that's how you missed your
flight.

TODAY

Fear not, The Syndicate always
builds-in a 24-hour cushion.

These jobs aren't *that* time sensitive.

You learned *that* the first time you
asked, "What can't wait 24 hours?"

Your handler answered, "very little."

Doffing top
and bottoms.
Prancing
onto the lanai
and into the pool.

You learned:

Short run, you get paid.
Long-run, she gets promoted.
Everybody wins. Again.

Fact is, you've begun to suspect...
          these un-planned 24-hour get-
to-know-your-handler interludes
are

14

more likely than not, pre-planned PERKS. And not merely for your happily misguided handlers.

You lament the years it took to arrive at that conclusion and make *another* mental note to *further* increase your B^{12} regimen.

And, in the short-short run, you're still in that SBC line, albeit a day later than expected. Now five from the front instead of 10.

It's moving along with inordinate efficiency, and you quickly ascertain why: "food," here, is expertly managed.

Fact is, many moons ago, before the masks but after the shoes/gels/liquids, SBC offered YOU the job of "Manager, Retail Food."

Mirroring large swaths of life itself, it seemed like a swell idea at the time. Praise be, The Syndicate stretched forth a grotesque tentacle just in time. With scant regret, you surrendered to its slightly gritty, infinite-tiny-plungered grip and... ah, well... suffice to say there's no way, anyway, you could have "managed" THIS:

A six-foot-five 120 lb., full-sleeve and neck-tattooed, fuchsia-coiffed tart:

Mistah Toasta, Tweaker Barista.

Hear ye, brothers and sisters, rest your device-addicted ocular orbs and feast instead your gaze upon Mistah Toasta whilst he WORKS his most-prized bitch – the SBC-exclusive, *Predator* Commercial Grade Toaster Oven. He takes NO PRISONERS. He moves those hot cross buns from counter to oven to sandwich paper to your tray in 30 seconds or less or this one's on SBC. And they haven't comp'd one in five years, and you can bet it's gonna stay that way or his name ain't Mistah Toasta.

He gives you the side-eye:
"What's good, Sweetie?"
"Triple Espresso."
"That's ALL?"
"Yep."
"What's your naa-aame, Sweetie?"
"F.C."

"TRIP-PIO for EFF SEEEEE..."
And that's exactly how he wrote it on the cup. You walk away, "like, lit-er-ally SMH." It is a damn good espresso, though. Not burnt or over-roasted in the least. Two sips and you're feeling cooler than a Jarmuschian fair tradecraft espresso assassin. You conjure (on spec, of course) SBC's new marketing campaign: "Drink our coffee. Walk through walls. Strike down Illuminati Gangsta Pimps. Inside their own barbed-wire ensconced, contract-goon-guarded hillside hideout."

Nah. Too subtle.

But still, was his motivation level commensurate with 623am on a random October Tuesday? Was he Meg Ryan "faking it?" Hamming it up for the boss?

Most importantly, does employee attitude effect the quality of roasted deli turkey and Havarti on gluten-free toast (tomato slice?).

Indeed, these things WOULD concern you...
IF you were "Manager, Retail Food."

Oh, but for The Syndicate's call. Has it really been 21 years? Perhaps it only *felt* more straightforward back then. You took that first call on your home phone in the middle of the night and your future first ex-wife asked, "WHO's calling YOU?"

As if it would have been more appropriate, at 330am on the dot, if the computer-generated voice had asked for her instead of you. It's possible, you know. She was quite ruthless, in her way.

Yes, a good soldier, you rogered up and followed instructions.

Ultimately, you found yourself on a fifth floor, ICW-overlook balcony. Turns out he was a minor player. So minor, in fact, he was downright expendable. And what you thought was a job interview was your first job. You always liked origin stories and vowed to write this one later. But 21 *years* later?

Hey, you're the one who asked, "what can't wait 24 hours?"

Today it's so much more complicated. Burners make the world go 'round. This world at least. Fucksake, you didn't even have A cell phone back then. Let alone four or five, all of which get trashed at job's end. There's one for your local contact, one for your handler, one for one-level above your handler in case your handler gets burned or whacked or quits, mid-job. So that's three right there – all flips. Took a while but you finally mastered the hang of flip-phone brevity-code texting with that whole 3 letters on every key thing. Except "9" which only has x and y.

Then there's the smart burners. Simplified secure messaging for the newbs but old schoolers won't touch them for ANY comms. You're sort of in the middle. You'll capitulate to using smarts for apps and apps only. Ballistics app. Maps app. Charge building app. Translation app. Facial recognition. Camera, Video. VPN. Code break and code make. Whole nine yards.

All connected to an (in-theory) secure cloud server that gets wiped after ever job. You Tom Shady the phones while The Syndicate (with tech support from Lady Arkancide) chlorox's the cloud.

Or so everyone says. Can't be proven either way. IF you've got a safe deposit box full of old phones in a Bermudan private bank, THEN they've probably got an (in-theory) double-secure triple-authentication-required back-up cloud with guaranteed (if necessary) deadman-switch destruction.

Blackmail works both ways and you like getting paid. On time.

You sip your *trippio* and, owing to your heavy saw palmetto intake, stroll toward your gate with just one pee break. Finding the men's room unnaturally empty, you naturally check every stall for miscreant lurkers.

Emerging unscathed by a flash-flooding urinal (ah, that old Fulton County chestnut), Gate C327 beckons – a mere two miles down the concourse. Plenty of steps to ponder in what potential past life you perhaps crossed paths with your nameless-by-nature handler...

Perennial befuddlement aside, it's nice to be part of a professional organization.

DEAD GRASS CARP

Floats bloated and red-eyed
pulled downstream
on Atlantic spring tide

Mr. Snook observes
"you don't belong here – it'll get too
salty"

DGC counters
"it's this skunkweed that's made me
sick"

Mr. Tarpon weighs in
"it's not the grass, it's you"

DGC relents
"it's ok, i can't breed and don't want
to live forever"

Mr. Shark glides alongside
"lunch is served"

YOU GRABBED 3

carousel CDs
one nine-inch &
two ministry

down 6
or 8?
Bancroft flights

out to Farragut seawall
creampuff ride w/
discman + tape deck adapter!

roommate who quit
     (then got married)
he's just up the way
in southeast PA

695 around Bulletmore
then 83 past Cockeysville
now on to Harrisburg

all the way
     down in it
burning inside
to a terrible lie

to what end
a precious Saturday night
in Camp Hill, PA?

@ 20, what point
to anything?

a fresh freedom thing.
signaling your little piece
admiring their big chunk.

alas, theirs overwhelmed
divorced in short order
but, then again, 1st at-bat,
        so were you

LOW TIDE

white-footed cat
stalks mangrove flat

pate`-buying master has gone

missus snook slithers
while mullets dither
their sunset arrives this dawn

VOICES

Not a team player.
Contributions zero.
Another grifter.
Straight minimums, around the horn.
Excuse me, Sir... but...

But nothing!
We've designed a special "debt
workout" program.
With just your kind in mind.
All you've taken,
you now return.
With interest.

Is this program "mandatory," Sir?

YES... DAMMIT!
It's MAN-DA-TORY!!
Perfect. Where do I sign?

WHEN GEN-X HUNS
RULED THE 619

lazy summer Friday
ST3 noon liberte`
monstermashrunswim

+ field day (yeah that's a mop,
cakeater)
your filthy, stinky
O's lockerroom

trucks, jeeps, hogs
odd 4-door beaters
roll out strong

down off Midway
oh, tasteful exotics
catch a glimpse
longlean ginger

flexing that
birdseye
maple-hewn
beach volleybutt

stretching that
taut
ring-pierced
belly

shaking those
proportion-
perfect
implants

grooving bentover
spreadeagle grind
to that AIC crunch

surfer chick, pin-straight mane of
crimson
lightly freckled shoulders
tossing tresses, to and fro'

blur of hair, metal guitarist
headbang
damming your river

can't recall her face?
doubt you ever saw it
surely never mattered

USED TO BE

we'd drive east on I-8
a little past
El Cajon
south side exit
service road and cut off
patch of open dirt
between two berms
around a bend
gravel pit
bonfire remains,
empty 40 oz's and old tires
but mostly
SPENT BRASS
east county's cap bustin' hotspot
frogs and marines and budlys
like you and me and lbd
slick willy (of lesser renown)
timmy d and the ivory elk
plus assorted
logan heights and
chula 'bangers
we all agreed
'twas righteous fields of fire
where no one bothered anyone
polite, armed society of
killers
and assorted aspirants
although one time
i did witness

titanium dave
put the boots to a punk
but not there – that one
was outside a strip club
decades down the road
confused my tall tales
on purpose?

OUR NEW TEAMMATE

i ask james why
joe comes off awkward
james explains
joe's taste-tested heavy mettle

panama '89
connors, rodruiguez, mcfaul and
tilghmann
down on the tarmac
joe and his boys
run to the guns

and shoot the bejeezus
out of everyone and everything
that might pose a (further) threat

then stand watch all night
over junked aircraft,
a trashed hangar and
body bags

i ask james why
joe lives in a trailer
size of a connex box
towed that sucker 40 hours
virginia beach to imperial beach

james explains
joe values three things:
shoot, move, communicate
if it doesn't fit in joe's trailer
it doesn't fit in joe's life

VOIDED EXISTENCE

off ramp launched into astral plane
you see your father's face in a
morning star then realize grounds
rushing up so fast if you don't fix this
quick you won't see your son or the
sun again that this'll be your last
sunrise but wow it took in the
curvature of the earth upward
viewing hurricane eyewall's inner
edge but instead you're facing down
and it's no way to die with your guts
splattered all over the yuma desert
so you get stable and pull and if your
main's a no-go you've got a reserve
but cutaway 1st and if #2 deploys as
poo well it's cliché but you've got the
rest of your life to figure out why

BEST INTENTIONS

she calls
she says

what are you waiting for
get over here

finish swinging
iron ball

she calls
she says

nevermind
i'm finished, too

your self-discipline's
bitter reward

GOING TO PIECES IN THE TROPICS

corner booth
corner bar
mis-understood
corner of the world
Oasis croons
the new-new Beatles

Play it again, Aroon... again!

girls on stage giggle
the one next to you
in the booth
smiles
it's good to be the king

*They worship The King here, don't
they?*
More Mekong, please.
And a Carlsberg. Singha "mi di."
And "leknxy" Mekong for Aung, here.

One more time, Aroon!

*Rxy tho, give it a rest will ya? We all
love that song, but it's getting
morose. S'posed to be a party.*

Aroon smiles
behind DJ glass
Angus chugs
Bon Scott snarls

bagpipes, 2nd verse

the girls on stage
        lime green bikinis
        glowing in the black light
        bouncing faster on stage
the ones in the booth
        and at the bar
        the ones already picked,
        all bobbing their heads and still
smiling

the boys
        all grins and slapping
        each other on the back
        laughing
        their fool heads off,
        telling war stories,
        comparing ink,
        new and old

it's good to be a knight

*They love their Knights here, don't
they?
More Mekong, please.*

And a Carlsberg. Singha "mi di."
And "leknxy" Mekong for Rose and
Yen and, of course, Aung, here.

at night's end
all aboard the *songthaews*
roll on back
to the *Bannammao*

Oasis lyrics flow through
        your head
as salty breeze flows through
        truck's bed
carrying blended scents of curry,
exhaust, trash, and perfume
and (of course)
a shared bottle

to help you remember to forget
as right as this all feels right here
is
as wrong as it'll all feel back there

NEVER MEANS MAYBE

out from under
target ship
kicking hard
for extract

three more minutes
one hundred more yards
then surface

but wait!
first one boom
then another
        – you think
        surface or
suck mud?

whichever
you can't remember

or even
that which you heard
or should have heard

doesn't matter much
        – you don't think

surface so appealing
up you go dreaming
nighttime glass interrupted

Maersk Line
slides past
blacking out your
familiar horizon

the 32nd street lights
are
simply
gone

six feet of line
feels like sixty when
your swim buddy's
six feet closer
than you

to
17,385 tons
plus
steel and screws

hand over hand
reel him in
and
here he comes
and
no one died
tonight

SOMETIMES WE'D FIGHT

just because
we thought
that's what
married people do

how dumb
we were
destroying something good

just because
we learned
from the wrong people

some things
you shouldn't learn
from people at all

those are the things
you should learn
from God

ESCAPE VELOCITY

Dreary room-thoughts fading fast,
pull door shut, walk down barracks
hall, out through main lobby, into
cold, damp and dark Honshu
evening.

Over bridge, past *The Rising Sun* hip-
hop clothing store – owned by?

[No, it's not Big Will with his classic
blue & white Dodgers ballcap – he
runs the Misawa rib joint.]

Pace quickens approaching
the train. All-aboard to wintry
Tokyo. Figure out change stops along
the way.

The symbols inexplicably make sense

– at least as much as these solo
excursions into the urban underbelly
of the Nippo-beast.

So different from where you came.
So different from where you went.

It's funny how your past and future
don't matter when the present

fully occupies all five senses
– and subconscious too.

No ruminating on regrets.
No plotting future days courses.

Just absorb and react
         to your moment at hand.

Off train, moth to flame, gravity-
drawn to flashing neon's inherent
promise of sex and booze and danger.
Pushing forward alongside teeming
anonymous masses. All here for
same attractions.

To forget what you left behind and
experience, feel, something,
anything, you seek and find club
dubbed:

Gas Panic! – bobbing your head, a
head taller than your tallest fellow
bobber, to driving riffs of what'll later
be christened "Nu-metal."

It's Korn and, apparently, they've
"Got The Life."

And young Japanese lovelies also
bang their heads – all in unison,

doffing their North Farce puffer
parkas, climbing up onto the bar,
gyrating in schoolgirl white button-
downs and blue-green plaid skirts.

Tojo's August 5th wet dream.

insuchaplaceatsuchatimeinsucha
stateofoutrightbuzzednessyounever
wantthismomenttoend

But alas, the lights come on and
the *Yakuza*-enforcer wannabes kick
you and everyone else out into the
damp, cold pre-dawn air and you find
your way back to the train station
and retrace all your steps back to
Atsugi – with the expert assistance of
at least one (perhaps more?)
exceedingly polite, exceedingly
inebriated local businessmen who
shook you awake at all the correct
transfer stops even though they were
drunker than you but at least they
could read the signs.

WE USED TO WALK

out side door
down woodchip path
to feral kitten alley

you'd pull
on a string
your wheel-footed
pup-pup plastic dog

denim bibs
where i could grab
both straps in back
where they came together

if
you were
to get yourself in trouble
by stepping off
the ferry landing dock
or

into orange avenue
or the busy street
running alongside
[was it kensington?]
coffee shop
straight into north island
main gate

opposite there, cornerwise
is where i met your mom
thirty years ago

which means
it's been about 25 years
since
we used to walk

ENTER SYNDMEN

Remember that bit with the 'Dant?
Or was it the 'Supe? The one where
he "invited" you into that special
program? That's right. The
MANDATORY one. For selfish
people. Who didn't know what they
wanted except they knew it wasn't
THIS. Yeah, that one.

This is that story.

They gave you a fake diploma and
said you were an officer. But you
weren't, really. You weren't even
really in the military. But everyone
thought you were part of The/Their
Program. Turns out they thought
wrong. You were part of The (Other)
Program.

Then, at a critical juncture, they pull you from training and stick you in a hospital. Something about cutting off your left leg at the knee if they don't get this nasty bug under control. You feel sick but not that sick.

Commandantè El Frowning and Major McNevermore visit, unannounced, in civilian attire. El Frowning sports an antique "I LIKE IKE" button. McNevermore, young, fashion forward and cause-driven, is c7-to-heels draped in black and grey urban camo performance fabric.

Unironically, a cryptic silk-screen ruins McNevermore's futureconcept stealth aspirations. It's a torso-size, laughing-so-hard-I'm-crying emoji with accompanying perimeter script:

Don't Advocate Sedition
Practice It!

El Frowning breaks the ice: "You'll do well to heal up here for a bit. We've got plans for you. And they start now."

McNevermore: "As of now, I'm your Commanding Officer. But it's an odd arrangement. The entire command is the two of us. And, although we're "in," we're still being screened. Your success depends on me and mine on you. Let that sink in."

El Frowning: "That's right, Wylde. We're evaluating the two of you as a unit. Think Strategically,
Decide Tactically,
Command... errr....
Inspirationally...?
Motivationally...?"

"We'll have to work on that. As a Highly Professional Organization, successful development of a catchy brand mantra is path ultra-critical."

"Going forward, you'll be graded jointly on your combined ability to employ taught skills to accomplish any given mission – plus any required improv *opportunities*."

"And please don't die. Fake causes of death are an entire, balled-up-at-the-home-office paperwork hassle we'd prefer to avoid. Not to mention a significant drag on NPV, IRR, ROI, free cash flow, etc. Any and all such impediments mightily displease the comptroller."

McNevermore: "You're not completing training with your class. There's no point. We now know you're tough enough. That's all we needed. The rest is a bunch of low-value, militaristic, team-building garbage. Surely these developments meet your approval. You were, after all, specifically screened for this role. You know, the whole "selfish, not a good Midshipman" thing. Besides, your mission set consists of entirely solo ops. At max, in cases of required redundancy, a pair. If we can produce another of your kind. But probably solo, because it's highly likely we'll be shut down long before we reach that phase."

You: "Wait...what, exactly, are you telling me?"

McNevermore & El Frowning [in unison]: "You aren't in the military. You never were. Not since

graduation. Maybe not even before
then. Who can be sure?"

You: "But what about you two?"

But they disappear and the drugs
knock you out again. You spend the
next year training. All over the USA
and sometimes beyond. Desert in
Arizona and New Mexico (avoid
sleeping on the ground – but good
luck finding a tree in which to hang
your hammock). Cold in Alaska
(never trust an inflatable – ground
pad, that is). Tropical maritime in
the Keys (water, water everywhere,
but not a drop to drink / instead of a
cross...). Woodland in Upper
Michigan and Upstate New York (it's
only flat and mild where you aren't).
Jungle in Panama (never ever, ever
sleep on the ground and if you find a
flat, bare rock that looks like a good
box spring for your ¾ length closed-
cell foam ground pad – remember,
flat and bare means floodwater
scoured).

McNevermore makes an occasional
cameo to "train and test alongside."
El Frowning sporadically drops in

(literally - by parachute –
demonstrably egotist ass that he is –
knowing how much you hate
skydiving) to observe and ramble
nonsensically about "OODA loops,"
"kill chains," and "national airspace."
There's no objective way to know
how you're doing. You assume you're
still "in it," because no one's bothered
saying you aren't.

You even pull off a few "practice"
capers with private security types.
Overall, these don't make much
sense and it's hard to tell what's
training and what's not. Some of it
might be both. The buckshot's
apparently authentic real when your
[REDACTED] militiaman blows out a
minor local warlord's (MLW) truck
tires and militiaman's pals yank
MLW out of the driver's seat, pistol
whip and throw him, zip-tied and
hogtied into the mangroves. When
the [REDACTED] police show up,
they don't much care – just throw
MLW in the paddy wagon and haul
him off to jail.

You wait for a *Deliverance*-style
admonishment: "don't you boys

never do nothing like this again."
But it never comes.

Eventually you cross paths with a
Derek Wince-type character. Except
female. Goes by name of Lauren
Stouffet (pronounced Stuff-it, NOT
Stu-fay). Her partner's Farley
Hunger - the real brains behind the
outfit. Everyone trying to make a
dishonest buck in parasecurity-
milintel world wants a meeting with
Stouffet and Hunger. And here you
are, thrown in their lap. Or they in
yours? Crossing paths time and
again, you come to view them as
Burroughs-esque "[sisters] in the
same dirty needle." Especially
Lauren – the randy cad. Farley?
Well, she's got her own "girl in 4E"
mystique. Their shadowy shell
company:

Twerkshire Báthory
"Not Sadism,
For Your Own Good!"

purchases, guts, repackages, and
flips – all with the evangelical
abandon that comes from knowing

"our only obligation is to the shareholders, Jack!"

El Frowning and McNevermore show up at another juicy juncture. Cali's Central Coast. An El Nino Winter. Big surf. A hundred miles north, the Hawaii boys just "discovered" Maverick's. In these dark days, pre-internet, you wait for the surf mags to hit the stands and stand in awe of the pics. McNevermore decides it's time to integrate your skills into a more conventional style op. And he's gonna lead from the front. As always, dammit. You board the 10-meter RHIB and the coxswain guns it on the high set.

Broken bones and canceled careers. Except theirs.

McNevermore chalks it to "pushing the envelope."

El Frowning concurs: "the price of doing business."

You "note it" and move on.

Training slows down, then grinds to a
halt. You're summoned to DC. El
Frowning and McNevermore in a
small conference room. Something
about budget constraints and
"sequester." It's all being shut down.
In-fighting on Capitol Hill.

El Frowning breaks the news:

McNevermore's off to grad school to
learn the fine art of deep voice
speaking about excruciatingly
mundane subjects, rendering
them...wait for it...

INFINITELY PROFOUND

And you? You're headed to SOS-P.

"What's that?" you say.

El Frowning replies: "Special
Operations Staff – Purple" ...it's a
multi-service staff where you dream
up reasons to create PowerPump
briefs and then brief them up down
and sideways to everyone until
you're blue in the face and none of it
will actually happen but we'll pretend
it's all very important and then when

something actually does happen the
operational units will pretty much
just wing it...errr...go with what they
got and then we'll all deploy to that
particular theater and get medals for
doing more (from scratch – even
though we've supposedly got all these
templates already in the can) Power
Pump in preparation for, and also
after, the operators go operating.
And no, it won't matter that no one
remembers you because you're just a
staff puke that no one pays attention
to (including the other staff pukes)
and you know just enough about this
mission planning stuff to be
dangerous and that doesn't even
matter because, as we discussed,
none of this will ever come to pass."

"But I didn't think I was even in the
military.
   I thought I was SPECIAL.
    Like, as in,
      REALLY, REALLY
    SPECIAL."

El Frowning stands and puts a hand
on your shoulder.

McNevermore stays seated, shaking
his head slowly.

Your heartbeat accelerates and your
face feels hot

McNevermore speaks slowly,
haltingly. Soothing baritone sliding
up an octave:

"You are and aren't.
Definitely ambiguous.
What we know for sure
        is your (former)
                Program's done.

Enjoy the SOS-P."

B-SIDE LOVE DREAM

our hot, raw demo track
aged into quirky little
passion project
b-side

but you weren't listening
anymore
well, not to *our* song
anyway

no matter we'd
built a life
on our combined will
and God's dreams

you casually discarded
our blistering riff
when it no longer fit
your song

and now i rummage
through dusty tapes
trying to exhume
and frantically resurrect

dead love's lost chord

A FUZZY MEMORY
(DID IT REALLY HAPPEN THAT
WAY?)

It's just a few days after those poor
student aviators who didn't know
how to land did what they did.

You're watching television on a
chamber of commerce autumn-in-
New England day.

Thad, a part-time Slayn Land
Institute tawking head speaks to the
camera:

"Nuke Tehran, Damascus and
Baghdad. Ensure this never happens
again."

You envision Thad pushing the
button with his marlinspike
proboscis, then riding a healthy
incoming tide, upriver to the weekly
pole dance contest at Enid's Endless
Sausage. Dorsal fin slicing a
midnight slick Potomac, he steadily
hums Les Claypool's opening bassline
to "Jerry Was A Racecar Driver."

THEY SAID IT WOULDN'T BE ALL OF THEM

newsperson said
little kids shot
in a dirty texas
bordertown

koward keystone kops
watched
them
die

seemed a big sad deal, all unto itself

but
we had no idea
how big or
how sad

first,
ammo went scarce
especially nine
and five-five-six
because
police and military *only*, bruh

then went the
deer rifle cartridges
two-seventy and thirty-aught-six
and even

twelve-gauge shells

the ninnies figured out
hunting ammo kills
just as dead
as
assault weapons

hording and stockpiling
now all the rage
fedgubmint jackboots
launch a mission
the one they've craved
round it all up

and if you thought those koward kops
at the school
showed their ass
let me tell you brother
when they went door to door
in some back o' beyond
texas brush
and tennessee hollers
and floribamississippiana swamps
they about shit themselves
but
you'd be surprised
what the good people
the rank and file
the salt of the earth

will do when their paycheck and
health insurance and retirements are
on the line

oh yeah
you know it
they stacked up and breached and
guess what?

the one and two and three and four
man
all got smoked with ol' man prepper's
double aught
but

the five and six and seven and eight
pumped yer boy fulla

yep, nine and five-five-six
turned out they're
damn useful

but only in the *right* hands
obviously

YOU WERE MY FAVORITE

always thought you knew
guess you didn't

or didn't
believe me
or
in me

did i seem insincere?
or
teach you to not trust
me?

did someone else?
and
if so
who?
because i'm quite sure
it wasn't me

but then again

i've been quite sure
about a lot

that simply
wasn't so

DEVIL'S BOATMAN

THURSDAY | OCTOBER27 | 2005 |
11:30PM

"You're way too cute to be single."

Aung
        doesn't love
        the dictated lines.
        Not her style
        but exercise's point.

Evening's top prospect
        flashes slight grin.
        His
        Eyes afire
        yet agenda-less.

Aung
        conversely,
        knows well her motive.
        Clarity's arrival
        at song's shift.

N.E.R.D.'s debut
        yields
        to old-school VH.
Murder for stage work.
Rock's perfect for room work.

Pretending to flirt.
Lies within lies.
Long
     Aung's
     stock in trade.

Righttimerightdaterightmouthrightg
aze.
Wives and kids and another
     burned up helicopter
     soft but genuine.
He belonged once,
     in his time.

"Private dance?"
"Yes."

Who said what doesn't
     matter
     deals a deal
     backroom or
     [private] booth.

On Wylde's lap
     she faces away.
Jet black hair
     down to his naval.
So pullable
     in another life
     in another time and
     place

        it was
        anyway.

No eunuch
        She
        thinks.
His
    left
        arm
            wraps.
Hand not cupping
            but holding

A photo of Her
        walking south
        crossing 61st
        east of Lex.

Yesterday's top
        and pants
            and heels.
Or day's before?

B-side: TARGET
Sweaty-suited bridgeandtunneloaf.
Currently ogling
            peroxide centauress
            Sunset
Yet rebuffing
        her "dance?"
                advance.

Cheaporwhippedorapussy?
      Anyorallthree
          Inspire
          Aung's inner Protestant
          (work ethic, that is)

Left calf
      brushes box cutter
      velcro'ed inside
      thigh-high black boot.

Diamond Dave's spoken word.
Final flourish
Eddie, Michael and Alex Unchained.

Aung stands and turns.
He smiles and it clicks, again.
Seven or seventy years
      smiles don't change.

"Finish, it's paid for."

Heartbeat pace, drum and bass
Billy Corgan's whining
Never a fan

Yet to Stand Inside Your Love
      suits this moment
      Perfect

Nostalgia for
        memories
        she doesn't have.

Does life flash
        before Aung's eyes?
        no.
FiveSenseFrontSightFocus.

Exit booth, snake through crowd
        to corner magnum 'Goose and
        her
        TARGET marked,
        [sadly] left on bottle watch.

"DoooodImdyinhereyouseguysallleft
me!"
Feigning victimhood
        yet victimizing
        long this targeted
        Oaf's
        stock in trade.

Wylde nods
        at him
        toward Aung.
"Ride of your life
        on this slow grunge fuzztone."
"Let's go, Big Boy"
        and it's off to
        the private booths.

Nose-ringed bull led
        stockyard to slaughterhouse.

Tony and Dino return with
        ladies in tow
        to swiftly settle deep
        into plush couch corner.

Wylde sips
        self-mixed martini
        lifts hips off couch
        extracts battery-less
        bbery from
        left front pocket.

"'scuse me, fellas
        gotta take this outside."
Dead device held to ear,
        he stands and walks off
As
Sunset and Dawn
        Occupy Wall Street.
All
        while in back
        Aung entertains.

Not a man
        but a TARGET
        she grinds
        its arousal

Furtive glance
  over right
  shoulder
  catches
Closed eyes
  that won't
  open
  again.

Walls rush in
Music fades out
Jet Black Mane
  & Thonged Thai Ass
Uncoil
  Violent
  counter-
  clockwise
  Twist.

Left elbow shatters
  left orbit.
Right palm fractures
  jawline.
Reversing flow
  left fist collapses
  TARGET's trachea.

Left Eye Blind,
  it gurgles weakly
  through busted jaw
  and

broken teeth.
Quick pivot | square-up,
        box cutter thirsts
        to cut
        and run.

Butonlyifnecessary.

It's not.
Aung's stiletto
        stomps
        its crotch.
No reaction.
Carotid pulse weakweakernothing.

Phase Two:
She cuts
        Herself

Notlikebefore:
MakeherselfUgly.

Nowthere'spurpose:
MakeherselfBleed.

TARGET's dead hand
        holds
        "his" box cutter.
while
Wylde holds
        his breath.

Listen!
There!

Aung's scream
        through din
        from back
        to front
        of
        [REDACTED FAMOUS
PORNOGRAPHER]'s *Rustler Pub* :

"Asshole cut me!"
(crude stripper-ease infused with
sing-song sexyThai-m lilt)

Grasping souvenir matchbox
        he strides into darkness

Right turn
        along building
        to 52nd Street

Cutting across
        West Side Highway
        to the bike path
        now double back south

Past *USS Intrepid* now empty
        dead men forgotten
        @Pier Eighty-Four Dog Run
        matchbox retrieved

Images torched
    ashes to Hudson
    no trophies tonight
    the box burns too.

Styx River Cruise Lines
    neon illuminates
    lonely ferry landing
    where a solo

Chiron's WaterCab
    24-foot center console
    bobs along the seawall.

"Teterboro," proclaims one Wylde X.
Bushman III to the shrouded,
roughly 6'5", 250 lb. mariner.

"You got it, Vik. You'll find an
appropriately nondescript domestic
beige four-door waiting at Edgewater
Ferry Landing. Please call me
Shirley."

Funny Names? Required fun in any
Highly Professional Organization.

PIMP

you search
while
he surrenders
secret keys to
a closed society
exclusive ownership
now lost

MEET STEVE CONDOR

elaborate stage
spotlight on
jeans and black turtleneck
a robbsy jobbins
clean shaven, muscular, crew cut,
wireless mic

(whisper progresses to screaming)

Ballistic Success Trajectory.
Say it.

Ballistic. Success. Trajectory.

Loud and proud.
BALLISTIC SUCCESS TRAJECTORY.
B.S.T. !
BEAST !!!

We can all launch ourselves on the
BEAST, if we only believe in our
Inner BEAST. In our cause.

It starts every morning with
brushing your teeth.

You MUST demonstrate
accountability to yourself.

I get up at 4am every morning, brush
my teeth and jump in a cold bath.

Then a hot bath.
Then back in the cold.

Then work the heavy bag for several
hours.

After that it's scheduled calls and
catching up on email until dinner,
then more of the same, then bed,
then do it all again.

Dammit, I've worked hard to build
this life for myself.

And it's all underpinned by the
BEAST.

So, if YOU want what I've GOT,
there's books
     and DVDs
          and download codes
               all for sale
               right outside those
               doors.

(points authoritatively to room's
rear, exits triumphantly stage right
to thunderous applause)

ONE'S A TRAGEDY, MILLIONS A STATISTIC

ants invade
post-termite treatment
to furiously feast
on *corpse de isoptera*
a dish best served
gassed

OF GETTING SHITCANNED

Your Quest. Your Risks.

And why you didn't make it *longtime*
at McDumpsterFire.

"data-driven"
"fact-based"
"yes, but that's anecdotal"

Stylish cultish
Madness.
You'd say, "let's do [X] and see what
happens."

They'd say, "pull data, build case,
present to top management."
[always in 3's]

You'd counter, "[Z], who runs
business unit [Y], likes [X] – why
can't we try it?"

"Things fall apart; The centre cannot
hold;
Mere anarchy is loosed upon the
world,"
[lines 4 and 5, William Butler Yeats,
"The Second Coming"]

None of your ideas got implemented.
None of your slides "made the deck."

Intuition has no chair.

In [REDACTED ICONIC,
HYPERHYDROTIC CEO's] Big
Conference Room.

"Did you test your hypothesis with
data?"

"No, because it's obviously true. We
can calibrate as we go."

Nope.

and Patton and Farragut didn't make
Partner.

16 years later, *deposed* in another
matter, you conjured a *reason*.

For your "Counsel. To. Leave."

Your easiest answer all day:
"I wasn't a very good consultant."

In *A Moveable Feast*, Hemingway laid
down his wickedest maxim:

"All you have to do is write one true sentence.
Write the truest sentence that you know."

Under oath, you spoke the truest sentence you knew.

COULD YOU DO WITHOUT?

a nice house
on a nice street
with a nice car
to drive
nowhere
worth going

a flat screen
on a big desk
with a view
to the rest
of your life

your kids' love
for giving them
what no one needs
or even wants

your kids' hate
for telling them
too late

you're only free when
freedom's all
you have

THE COST OF 2ND CHANCES

"The only thing we're sure of is we
didn't get our money's worth.

You
       always wanted
       to do
       whatever you wanted
       to do
       whenever you wanted
       to do
                       it.

So, we're granting your wish.
Mostly.

The Faustian part of the bargain is
what comes with all that freedom.

Advance knowledge that we can and
will rip it all away on no notice.

And, yes, we have ways to ensure
you can't evade us."

14 years later, you find yourself,
again, waking up in a hospital bed.
With a sore ass. And McNevermore,
again, seated, looking at you from
across the room.

"Sorry, Wylde. It's all very necessary. The discomfort won't last too long. Maybe a few days, max."

"What have you done to me?"

"We've implanted a tracker very high up in your colon. Almost to the lower intestine. It can't be removed. Well, I guess it can. But that would risk a 99% chance of impotence and a 99.9% chance of a colostomy bag."

"I like my chances."

"How's that?"

"Obviously, you didn't live the last 14 years inside my head."

"Perhaps not. But we've seen enough of the outside to know what makes you tick. Your divorce, for example. What a shitshow. At what point did you possibly imagine the judge NOT hammering the snot out of you on that deal? He's on our payroll, too, you know. You really made it all too easy. Anyway, there's a phone charging on the side table. About the

time your mind limbers up, it'll be
ready to go."

With that, McNevermore gets up and
walks out the door. A nurse walks in.

"Another shot?"

WAKE UP BRAIN WAVES – THE
ESSENCE OF

details distilled
motions reduced
thoughts purified
life renewed

leaves fall
you sweep
leaves fall again

while you sleep
trains chug past
as do stars
effortlessly

if you call
knowing i'm not
in
the credit's still yours
sans conversation

finally, nothing's
holding you back
better get started
eventually you'll eat
then meat sweats
will stop you

regularly modeling
deep thinkers
you irregularly
think deep

DOOMSDAY GEPPETTO

Driving south on U.S. 1
through that vast mangrove thicket
Florida City to Key Largo

No Man's Land

It dawns on you now,
their Weakness:

Belief in

Their monopoly
on one thing:
Violence

Helo spins up

Whine then thump then roar
southwest
Green and black and blue and blur
now fast

Toward them

Wishing you were somewhere else
Realizing you're already there
Placid landing
Pristine golf green

Radio Free Cudjoe said
be ready to fight
The Good Fight
you yearned for

Armed Anarchist Uprising
resorts, hotels, Navy Base
all under siege

Who fired first?

Hard to say, here and now

FEVER DREAMS OF GRAND-EUR DELUSIONS

BETWEEN|
THURSDAY|OCTOBER27|2005|
ANDTODAY

You wish
     you'd missed
     that call.
Spamsung-stock
     ringtone piercing
     Danny Carey's turned-up-to-11
drum solo.

Despite high frequency
     hearing loss.
And your cerebrum's doleful dwelling
on the reams of mandatory
disclosure your soon-to-be-ex-wife's
attorney insists you provide by 4pm
TOMORROW, always tomorrow.

A sexed-up hint of Caribbean lilt.
But other inflections, too...

Is it an Irish brogue with a wee bit o'
clipped Trans-Caucasus?

If your RAM wasn't so full of jack-
hammer drumming

you might connect it to
something in the ROM.

She's Artris Sub Clavian.
She's new on-air talent.
She's with Miami's WLYE and "how
are you doing this lovely South
Florida day" and "can [she] stop by
around noon tomorrow and interview
[you] for a piece [they're] airing on
"the new stars of Independent
Investment Research?"

Never shy of talent, or prospective
star treatment, you inform her
tomorrow's fine, and does she plan to
take pictures?

Yes, and now
        time's arrived to deep-clean
this den of ill-deeds and [empty]
Giant Squid Rum handles.

2MINUTESLATER

resume daily ritual
self-flagellations

respite from your Camus
        meets Pychon

[punched-up w/sub-fatal dose of
Ludlum]

life of understated brilliance
world-wide reknown

all asset classes
and classy asses

NEXTDAYNOONISH

Ding-dong.
Through just-replaced front-door's
side-pane of barely-frosted glass
        a dark-haired
        dark-skinned
        white jump
        -suited
        unmistakably female figure.

Turn it down?
Turn it up?
Turn it off?

Pantera to Trick Daddy?
Would too quick a switch
        feel contrived?
Dime prevails.

Deadbolt left, handle down, door
swings outward (hurricanes)

and what to your wondering
eyes should appear but, a species
unique to the 305: the elusive
Caribé-queen dominatriarch, clad
head-to-toe in current season's
Kardash-a-Klone Kouture

accompanied, not by a
motivated team of eight undersized
reindeer, but a consumed-with-
malign-intent, yapping Yorkshire
Terrier in studded, pearlescent
leather harness.

Outside of hurricanes and civil
unrest
you never enjoyed local TV
news. But now consider
reconsidering it.

"Oohhh...I LOVE "Becoming"
that core riff
sets me head a' bangin'."

"You know your groove metal
but
how old were you
whence dropped
Far Beyond Driven ?"

How she knew
        how to say
        what
        never crosses your mind.

"No Mon, I'm a wee bit older than I
look
        and oh, by the way
        I'M INTERVIEWING YOU."
"Hey, no probs
        I like groveling
        and being bossed around
        ask my ex-wife."

"Indeed and
        we'll get to that in the
interview
        now please turn around
        I must inspect the merch."

Your A-HA moment:
        a newscaster she isn't.
Handlers know weakness,
        and she is well-trained.

"THWAACK!!!" Sonofabitch.

Dad always promised
        Principal Cotton Mather
        would ONE DAY
        break his paddle

on your ass.
Down in the boiler room.
Like back in HIS DAY.

No, NOT a newscaster.
Yet, no misanthrope
        elementary administrator.

Despite
        Ken Griffey, Jr. swing.

What stings more
        her hand
        or hypodermic
        or getting fooled AGAIN?

New boss?
        same as the old boss.

+24

warm breeze
flutters blinds

side-table grapefruit juice
poached eggs
fresh-buttered sourdough toast
(*but is it gluten free?*)

white linen
mosquito-canopied

king-size four poster
renders mere comfort
a filthy mind's projection
your mighty despair
one missing piece
then again, that Yorkie did bark
excessively
and once again you mentally note:

It's nice to be part of a professional
organization.

HOW I KNOW I FAILED AGAIN

What's to say that's gone unsaid?
Scarcely a thing.
Nevertheless, I'll replay the message.
For the inattentive.

Freedom is on the ropes.
If you haven't heard,
I'm sorry.
If you have, I'm not.

We did this to ourselves.
Revel in
the "new normal."
No one is coming.

Because we fell asleep.
And missed Cairo.
A nighttime lapse.
Our final undoing?

Escape at hand
Is night's
quiet comfort
Our ultimate demise?

We floated quietly.
Dreaming freedom,
Walking overland,
We sneak North.

DRINKING

you won't quit
for fear
of becoming

un-beguiling
and

i won't quit
for
same reason

PATHWAY RESET (NEURAL VARIETY)

when you didn't
call me
i didn't care
when you didn't
love me
i didn't dare
not
call you back

if i climbed a mountain
you swam an ocean
when you drove fast
i walked slow

how on earth
and why?
did we
ever
collide

you got bored
being my lord
i got tired
being your serf

together
we flatlined
in parallel

WHY I MISSED COMMUNION – AGAIN

Faithful troop of solemn dissident
right-wingers

Filing in
to that forbidden rite
Of Latin Mass
at [REDACTED]'s house

But the Padre went off script
Something about the abundance
Of spiritual movies on *Scamazon*

Which only made you think of
Whorin Greedos Trampez
All gooey lips and plastic chest

Holding tight
To her phallic starship
on last night's
Sucker Quarrelsome

Did you hear she's a helo pilot?
A bravestrong girlboss
Ready to ride

El Jéfe's rocket
Into space.

Un-ZEN

thoughts seeking
analysis
ideas needing
explanation
stories requiring
exposition
speech mandating
context
actions demanding
apology

FEVER DREAMS OF GRAND-EUR DELUSIONS (VERSE II)

Head throbs inafog.
Needadoubleespresso.

Staff works 24/7/365.
Whether Poorski's here or not.
Make call.

On-time and under-budget.
No sign of deliverer.
3X and gone – the way you like it.

Elixir left on tray outside the hand-
carved, Tiki God-in-profile,
mahogany door.
First sip.
Mind clear and time to assess:

You harken back to Ms. Flouncey
Turpentine.

One Shining Moment. Single file line,
waiting for the bus ride return to
Shay's Rebellion Elementary, feelin'
froggy after a week of machete blade
avoidance training at *Goalie Mask
Pond 5th Grade Camp*, pulling that
store brand bottle of *Croke* straight
outta your ultimate temptation, the

"counselors only" wooden crate,
popping top on a rusty nail head,
offering it to your ONE, TRUE
UNDENIABLE, UNREQUITED,
and (perhaps, in its time?)
FORBIDDEN LOVE.

And watching her she smile and
drink it down, saving you a taste.

Your perpetual chase.
Your perpetual weakness.
This time, last time, every time.

That feeling you get when you get
away with what feels righteous and
justified and flips the bird at
THE MAN and THE SYSTEM.

And you make a woman happy.
Doing it.

Between meditation hour one and
two, your mental playlist shifts,
nudging further into artsy
indulgence.

Fincher's *Fight Club* closing credits-
track rolls.

En-suite intercom squawks:

"Meestah Vik, Meestah Poorski, will see you at dinner. 30 minutes from now, main dining room."

You ponder the punchline.

Chaos, Theft, Murder, Mayhem?

Subtle human rights abuses masquerading as squishy humanitarianism?

Or merely racketeering, fraud and assorted financial crimes?

Your closet's been raided, the booty transferred here: Linen trousers – check. Sockless brown *Faerygamo* drivers – check. Tastefully rebellious *Robby Grimm* floral print shirt – check.

Maybe not a killer, maybe not before dawn (but feeling your Mr. Mojo), you dress smart and walk on down the hall.

Past the replica Farnese Hercules. Past the original Rubens sketch thereof.

Frankie greets you from behind the teak bar. Picture of house-staff dedication in perma-stained, double breasted chef's coat with green embroidered "Francis."

"Lighten up" traverses from prefrontal cortex to lips and tongue ... then reverses course, unvocalized.

A diminutive, olive-skinned gentleman, Frankie, it's rumored – is at least connected if not actually *made*.

"Vik, mi paisano! What are you drinking these days?"

"*Guevara Chi Lumumba's Rum Revolution,* double, one BIG ice cube, Key lime wedge. On the rim."

Presence behind painted-bamboo partition *ukiyo-e* of tiger stalking maiden, now emerges a Mandarin-collared, *Shanghai Fabulous*, floral, knee-length green dress housing one...

Mr. I.M. Poorski. In drag.

"Vik, sooooo good to see you, sooo glad you made the trip. You see, it's a Gift From The Universe. A once-a-century blow. The Jenny Jameson of tropical cyclones. Cat 5 PLUS. Bearing down on Richards Cay, specifically tracking right up Keef's Creek. There'll be chaos and crises ready-made for your expert expat exploitation. ToOurMutualBenefit. Mine at significantly less risk and higher return. But you've never quibbled about your level of risk. Or your return. I assume you won't this time. How's 10% on a metric tonne of [REDACTED COMMODITY REPORTEDLY NOT CONSIDERED AN ASSET CLASS BY BARTON BIGGS]?"

Your (rusty) consulting case-study quick math yields your [prospective] take at $6.2 million. Depending on liquidity day's spot price.

All that's required is

A) survive a Cat 5 PLUS and
B) gracefully, stealthily, surreptitiously, illegally, take and transport slightly more than 2000 lbs. of...

C) ah, well, who cares...?

"I'm IN!"

HOW I KNOW I FAILED AGAIN
PART II

hyacinth
floats past fast
canal current
carries its load
better than you ever
could or did

cat 5 floodwaters
ride twice a day
floodtide's stallion
house stays dry
until it doesn't

try to stem, to no avail
black dog
knows, sits, waits
gut-worm
killing chlorine's
easier drinking
when pool's full

sad men clinging
sudden turning
happy when it's gone

WORDS

facing death
feel
virtual, impotent
in paradox and truth
they, themselves
are
immortal

edges enchant
alphas and omegas
seafoam, meet rocks
violence repeats, repeatedly
neither much cares

WORKPLACEVIOLENCE
KILLSTHESPIRITWORLD

owing to
your intense supervision
and corrective nature
we err infrequently

inside our
relentless march
toward middle-upper
management

disciplined
grand theft mandatory
round-the-clock
availability

undistracted
by anything
important
we render unto Caesar

our unclothed emperor's
unauthorized daydream
indiscretions unindulged

YOUR EPIC DISCONNECT

release from appropriately
nuanced corporate-ese

and minimally inflected
inoffensive industry jargon

offspring off sprung
detailed - perhaps to a fault?
planning begins for

PERMANENT PERIODIC ALIMONY

ticks and leeches
feign disinterest while
head shot zombies
shuffle shabby rentals

tepid hope, modest ambition
blind justice
fuels sputtering ignition
under contempt's duress

lifelong conditioning aside
how could you?
thrive incarcerated
shoulder wheel, cover nut

your epic disconnect?
euthanized, metastasized
merciful fait-accompli
life's sands spilling
hourglass bottom filling

MISSION ACCOMPLISHED

I [HAD] A DREAM

playing bass
in a band called
campus radical
we score
a hit single

the deep state (we are all)

charting in
beijing
pyongyang
havana
but mostly

dc

SWITCH FLIPPED
BREAKER TRIPPED

you know what's right
       this thing
       your destined
       intention

they know, too
       this same thing
       their most
       secret fear

you've overcome
       atmospheric
       friction before them
       [will they ever?]

now sense time's shift
       to otherworld
       last stage drops
       next stage fires

they rearview-vanish
       truth noose tightens
       knowing they'll never
       catch up

revelation's genesis
spurred by
steady refrain

it's all your fault

but this time
        you finally
        asked yourself
        if it's possible
        that none of it is

not because
        you knew
        the answer

        but because
        you knew

        the answers
        the statements
        the questions
        the exhortations

didn't exist and
        you
        hung
        up
        the phone

FUTILITIES'
EXPLOSIVE RESIDUE

INT. SHABBY OLIVE DRAB TENT

soldiers mill about
states of dress and undress
naked to PT gear
to full combat loadout
to hybrids of all 3
flatscreen tuned (as always) to

GLOBAL SENSATIONAL BREAKING
NEWS FLASH

wide shot, desert wasteland
now zoom
13 torch-bearing,
tie-die shrouded,
hooded druids
circled around
pyramidic pile of
naked, decapitated
bloody-anused
once human
bodies
now afire
cut back to the desk

GLOBAL SENSATIONAL BREAKING
NEWS FLASH SPOKESMODEL
(ultra-serious, yet soothing baritone)
The genocide happening in Leeward
Alf Laylah Wa Laylah Archipelago is
believed to be orchestrated by a
terrorist mastermind calling himself
Blast Radius.

Brigadier Admiral Jock Rogers,
speaking from his command tent in
occupied Windward *Alf Laylah Wa
Laylah* Archipelago has promised an
overwhelming response.

INT. MUCH NICER OLIVE DRAB
TENT

overly decorated
clean-shaven
square jawed
grey-haired

BRIGADIER ADMIRAL JOCK
ROGERS
(sternly, resolutely)
We WILL pacify Leeward *Alf Laylah
Wa Laylah* Archipelago.

INT. SHABBY OLIVE DRAB TENT

soldiers continue to mill about

ORTIZ
Lewis, holy shit, you seeing this?
Look what Blast Radius did to those
poor fucks. What a fuckin' mess. And
now Rogers says WE "will pacify that
city." What the fuck is he smoking?
"WE," my ass...

LEWIS
Yeah. Fuck that guy.
It won't be him getting beheaded,
broiled, and buggered.

ORTIZ
And not in that order, either.

WOODSON
Will you two shut the fuck up?
I'm trying to listen to this shit.
Fuck's sake. 12 years of war and it's
all gone pear-shaped.
At least at the start it was obvious
WHO, EXACTLY needed a bomb or
two up their ass.

EXT. CAFE - DAY

12 YEARS PREVIOUS
WINDWARD *ALF LA YLAH WA
LA YLAH* ARCHIPELAGO

Peaceful, Mediterranean-looking
seaside corniche.

Patrons enjoying red wine & espresso
w/small plates of grilled octopi,
hummus, naan & olives.

Military jets roar high overhead.
Patrons look up.
Then back to their conversations.

POV shifts, overhead from 30,000
feet, zooming in, downward, fast as a
bomb falls.

Back and forth, this view to patrons'
POV several times - closer on faces
each time. Closer to earth each time.

Massive explosion, bomb's POV.
We live inside a fireball.

TO THE GRINDERS

does it make your life
worthwhile
will it make your death
meaningful
did it make your birth
noteworthy
???

permission

don't wait
for it
just be free

if you insist
on waiting

there it is

eleven lines up
take your gift
and run

EVERYTHINGABOUTYOUISFAKE

two pit-mixes trying to pull you out
door like a dog team of old but first
you punch in set-alarm code, open
interior house door, open garage
door, close interior house door
behind you, walk out open garage
door, then punch-in code to close
garage door and finally walk down
limestone-pavered driveway,
tripping over errant slabs (pushed up
by black olive roots) and turn left
and down street, dog team now
actually pulling you, sun at your back
and into west wind, it's that time of
morning when lots of folks dog-
walking so big black male half-lab
gotta piss on every mailbox post and
smaller brown and white amstaff she
gotta copy whatever he does so you
don't get very far very fast but get
you do and then you see HER: she's
just pulled into the driveway of the
house you call the porno house
because it's a big blocky brutalist
chalk-white two-story with porthole
circular windows and there's always
two cars out front an ebony *Escalate*
with 24" rims and an onyx *Fauxdi*
convertible but this platinum-blonde

chick who just pulled up she's driving
a canary yeller *Posche*
SansUtilityVehicle and she's
naturally petite but with a big giant
fake rack and fake ass and hair in a
ponytail and yoga-ready pink
athleisure attire with zipper pulled
down just so and she gets outta
driver's seat and goes around to back
lift-gate and opens it and there's a
bunch of luggage type things there
and school backpacks, all with boy-
type markings of baseballs and camo
and she loads up her shoulders with
three bags per and struts to the front
porch in a huff (it's such a bother)
and dumps 'em all and then stomps
back to driver's seat and backs up
and out of there and all you can think
is everything about you is fake:
boobs, ass, hair, face but especially
your status as "mother" – ain't no
mother treating your son's stuff like
that as you dump it on dad's porch
for weekend visitation and off to yoga
class where you're probably banging
your instructor and maybe your
personal trainer, too – hey why not
both at the same time – you tarted-up
caricature of a retread gorgon

111

FLOWER SHOP DUDE

always does
what you tell him
even if
it's a bad idea
those pay
too

MUSE GEN-EXISTENTIAL

You're putting up outdoor Christmas
decorations.
For your new wife.

Your ex-wife drops off your [time-
shared] son.
For "visitation."

She [that being said ex-wife]
comments:
"You never did that for me."

You reply:
"You never compensated me
appropriately."

She says:
"Fuck off."

You think:
"Instead of using my money to buy a
brain
You bought tits and personal
trainer."

You brush and floss and get in bed.
You recite your MANTRA.
Your AFFIRMATION.

You've devoted your life to nothing.
And it's finally in your grasp.

You set yourself
adrift like Bligh

Tax paid.
Time trade.

I quit my way
to victory.

Deciding
my style wasn't yours
Your timeline
wasn't mine
and

Implied contracts
aren't.

Seeking
[not] judgements,
but
questions:

Is time spent
doing no harm
      wasted?
      in itself,
      harmful?

Your infinite 12-D chess boards.
Your conjured manifestations,
seeded in dreams and germinated in
reality's fragmented perceptions
don't –

Trap Me.
AnyMore.
Than they need
Trap You.

Alas,
traps keep us
on the rails.
sans,
we taste
freedom.

But it'll cost ya.

DISPOSABLE CULTURE
FEEDING TUBE

sing-along drunks
tiki bar sunsets
white sand umbrella
imbibing nonsense

back's to entrance
never ideal
let it slide
one time only
just be mild

happy accidental
observation post enabling
furtive glances to far bank
mangrove-lined creek mouth

wife's colleague's husband's
man-crush drones on
breathy, rapid, barely audible
though not wholly unpleasant

but a bit of awareness
please?
Mr. IIT-pedigree
focus intently
and you'd possibly

witness

a raccoon pawing
his plot
of mud skimmed, low tide
far shore sand

baby, don't you know
if we'd left
fifteen minutes ago
we'd be home

screwing

what i'm trying
to convey
is how to
play

your role

over the top
freak on fast
or die slow

no permits required
no daytripper
       turístas allowed

BRO COUNTRY IN-VERSE

7
70
700
You choose
Each path ends alike

7 like you've been

70 like you heard you're supposed to
when there's no tomorrow except
after first 7 when you're sick,
medicated and hospitalized into an
unavoidable downward spiral
careening toward a predictable finale
that doesn't care how much we all
love brave fighters who never give up

700 where you barely notice until
last 70 you're slowly ground to dust
by forces you can't see except when
bills arrive announcing how sick you
are, how much you owe, payable in a
future you won't see – while your
loved ones pay now but instead with
time they don't have – at least not
any more than you had at their age
when you thought time was all you
had but turns out you had no time
at all

TRUST MISPLACED

[redacted] called
out of the blue
the [redacted] industry
it's so misogynist
is it –
or do they just
not tolerate
bitches?
[redacted]
doesn't call anymore

ODE TO MY POCKET PITTIE

large of head
small of brain
thrash designer pillow
with overt malice
and outright contempt

WHY WRITE POETRY?

money – exes take
fame – attain to forsake
sex – turns out fake

verse?

etch it 24-7
while your conscious brain
pantomimes
attentiveness

explode your plastique
dyna-mind
your wretched state
truth thru fiction
essence via façade

no rules
strict coherence gone
only ensure
your words

gut punch

DICE, NIETZSCHE, WHITMAN & YEATS ALL WALK INTO A BAR

you never blankety
blank
my blanking blank
anymore
(she wails)

indeed, there's only scant
pathetic begging
and pleading
one sailor can take
(inherent callousness aside)

resolutely we march
straight to the bedroom
bent over footboard
pleated red tartan
(seduce me, oh Ghost
of Halloweens Past!)

compelled to placate
no slouching allowed!
satisfy your rough beast's
vile demands
(w/copious lubricant
and Irish whiskey)

RIVER RHYTHM WITNESS

end-of-outgoing
jetty sheepies
wintertime barnacle munchers
how do you not break a toof?

sharp-eyed heron
skims river's surface
mullets jump in response
uneaten, yet again

worrying their way
through ancient gateways
while ice queen snook
lurk silent and stealthy

DAWN STRUT

each sunrise
same walk
down wash
into south wind

harem on his mind

we let him once
he got cocky
we let him twice
he got dead

CIRCLE JERK

bearded vet
virtual therapy session

Q: do you consider yourself mentally
tough?
A: only when things are easy

i've written some
poetry – i think it helps

please share

i have a tiny caulk
     gun
     own and embrace
     its smallness

INAPPROPRIATE!

[minor tantrum
ensues & ebbs,
verse continues]

i have four kids
     same
     babymama

i guess she liked
     diminutive

sealants
('til she didn't)

spontaneously
SWAT
simultaneously
breaches

front door explodes
flying shrapnel strikes
black dog, off chain
wild abandon barks
circling 'round
kitted up flooding goons
"down, down, get the fuck down !!!"
path critical violence
forces compliance

you'll find out
who, why, and why now?
while flex-cuffed on your face

main concern:
will they shoot black dog?

"does that dog bite?"
"are you an asshole?"

BOOMYIP

[No animals were harmed by these
thoughts or the reading or writing of
them.]

WLYE BREAKING NEWS
bearded vet and black dog
down in the 561
more at 11

lesson?
        no feedback
        whilst work's
        in progress
lest ye
        risk stunting
        creative
        process

KOANHEAD

who is my master?
whom you obey

what is my purpose?
what you are

where do i find power?
where you lost it

when will i die?
when you no longer live

why do i sin?
to consciously justify your
subconscious guilt

how will i know?
when you no longer ask

RIGHTHERE MAN

TODAY, GATE C327

You expected greater drama, but no,
there it is, just a few more steps. You
find a seat with a clear view of the
bored boarding board, sit and wait –
but not long. A presence in your
peripheral. You look up and to the
right – with just your eyes. Well, well
– The Syndicate unveils a new trick:
your handler, evidently, is traveling
with you for a stretch. You lament
your corroded surveillance detection
skills. She sits an appropriate
distance away and flashes a wry grin.

Boarding commences and reaches its
inevitable conclusion without
incident. Except she's sitting next to
you. This won't do. You'll be forced
to talk shop the whole 3-hour flight.
Maybe even "run through the deck."
But the flight's full. There's no fixing
this travesty.

And only one movie offered:

A Holiday Block Buster: *Story Time*
(West Side Variety).

Directed by *that guy.* You know.
That guy who did not one, but *two*
movies making aliens uncool. Flying
across the moon. Devil's Tower in
your living room. And let's not start
in on sharks. Or dinosaurs. The
reason *that guy*'s movies don't age
well: his whole rep is based on
cutting edge tech. And when it's no
longer cutting edge... neither is his
film.

After two hours of squirming
  and struggling
    for meaning
      your thoughts run
    a loop of:

"Who would actually *want* to be
involved in this steaming pile of
dogshit?"

You cryalittleinside and verbalize to
your seatmate:

   CHIIINooooo ....
   KILL ME, TOO ...
    please....?

"Awww... c'mon, Ruprecht [The
Syndicate promised one day you'd
get to pick your own aliases], was it
really that bad? Did you *never*
believe in romance?"

You reply: "Sure, of course I did.
Back when I gave a shit. Back before
I realized what's true and's got value
now, versus, say, *tomorrow*. You
know, NPV-style."

"And, what, pray tell is that?"

"A couplatings:
        black coffee
        red wine

        Pattaya Pros
                in blacklight glow

                swaying gently to
                'Wonderwall'
                (or White Zombie)

                as choosing time
                draws near"

"You sick bastard."
"I'll tell you what's sick."
"I think you already did. You."

"Maybe. But at least I'm not..."

16 permutations of crazy
Permutations of crazy 16
Of crazy 16 permutations
Crazy 16 permutations of

"Enough!
This farce has reached its end!
    I see where you're going here.
        A 64-word title that's a
        [shitty] poem
            unto itself,
        wrapping, intertwining,
          literally
       embodying
            your entire
       ethos."

"Ethos? You think I'd stoop to
having an *ethos*?

"Indeed, you would. Albeit a futile
one. It's as if you WANT to fail.
Intentionally Obscure.
Purposefully Incoherent.
Utterly Inscrutable.
Absolutely Incorrigible."

"Ahh... you think I'm merely trolling the Beats? A bit of Howling on the Road to the Western Lands sort of thing? Well, I can assure you, ma'am, this is nothing of the sort."

"Let me ask you a question, MISTER Faulkner."

"Shoot"

"Why'd you *really* take this job?
Why not just avoid this nonsense altogether?
You don't seem to like it anymore.
You don't seem to like me."

"You're right. I don't. I like the money. More to the point, I need it."

"Child support?"

"Some of it. But also, to pay off that insufferable pop culture icon, ONOB. Filed a lawsuit against me after I outed him for [REDACTED].

Judge didn't rule in my favor."

"Had to do with [REDACTED]
going to [REDACTED]
and saying [REDACTED]
about [REDACTED]."

"Seriously?"

"No. I mean, yes. Seriously. Would I lie to you, after all these years?"

"Are the redactions part of the settlement? The judgment?"

"Neither. I just don't think you'd 'get it.' Or you'd continually interrupt me with nonsense gossip-column tidbits, thereby degrading all impact the story might have had. So, I leave out the details. Gives you zero to play off, amIright?"

"If you don't mind ruining your own damn story.
        And humiliating your audience.
                Simultaneously."

"I know. It's no mean feat. Consider it my *special genius*. God, wouldn't that sound better *en Francaise* ?

By the by, did you see the ad where
the sexy-matron of vaguely Tex-
Mexian descent tells you what
detergent best gets your whites the
whitest?

Did you think it was racist?

Like, subliminally, she's your
cleaning lady or maybe your Freud-
dream nanny?"

"Or, in your case, R.F., your Long-
Lost Aztec Auntie-by-Marriage Who
Sleeps Over?"

"Easy there, Sister... don't make me
think The Bad Thoughts..."

> *Off your payroll*
> *Time to read*
> *Got an Scamazon bot*
> *Who hears my thoughts*
> *Slips Mental Mickeys*
> *Til I bleed*

Her expression jerks you back to
reality.
     You've seen it before.
          Many times.
               That look of

"I really want to *get it*,
but I'm not sure I do."

You want to explain that you're not
sure you "get it," either.

That it's not about spelling something
out.

It's about
    the feeling
        of feeling "bad"
            about something,
    but also
        feeling
            like you don't feel
                quite
                    bad
                enough.

You know someday she'll have a
better handle on English along with
the requisite cultural context to
grasp the nuance.

And that's when she'll say

"It's nice to be part of a professional
organization."

But, for now, you sail a new tack...

"Enough about me.
Did I ever tell you how I came to
"own" this
          cur
              curled
                      up
                          at my feet
otherwise known as
Black Dog...?

"Cur'? Isn't that a little pejorative
for your best friend?"

"Fair enough, but HE didn't *really
know* I was talking about HIM, did
he? I mean HE's a DOG."

"You cruel bastard!"

If you're soft
Live hard
If you're broke
Live rich
If you're dumb
Live smart
If you're bored
MAKE IT INTERESTING

Reverie broken; you craft your
retort:

"Cruel?
Did you know, I once thought
of becoming
a Life Coach
but
realized I'd have
to talk with
people
at appointed times.
Everyone's too busy
To talk at the RIGHT time.

Like when I interviewed Black Dog
for *Doggy Doo Digest*:

Timing is everything, and Black Dog
was at peak intellect.

Sadly, the "Triple Delta" went belly
up before it went to print."

"Is this an avoidable story?"

"No."

BLACK DOG:
THE LOST INTERVIEW

Ruprecht: *"Black Dog, do you ever tire of asserting your dominance?"*

Black Dog: "Shut the fuck up and sit down."

"Do you enjoy working jigsaw puzzles?"

"C'mon, man! My life doesn't suck that bad. Yet."

"You're a notoriously randy lad, remarkably so, given your, err... condition. Who's your favorite adult film star?"

"Well, it is hard to choose just one. But I *can* tell you, in no uncertain terms, I can't abide Don Hairemy."

"Tell me about Kobe Bryant. I hear you two had long-standing beef. Did you clear it up before the, uh... accident?"

Black Dog: "Naw, bruh – you're thinking Mike Vick. You know, I can't remember the name, but I'm gonna give you a quote. Maybe you can find out who said it."

Ruprecht: *"What's the quote?"*

"[He] got mad flava just oozin' out of him."

"That's a helluva a line. Any idea what year?"

"All I remember is that it came from the world of hip-hop. Or maybe old school funk. Could have been George Clinton. Or Ice Cube. Maybe Jay-Z. Royal rhymin' lyrical blood, no doubt. And when he took Brandy to his high school prom, he became my favorite NBA player before he even had a contract. Mad Flava, indeed. His rookie year, 1996-97, I watched every Lakers game possible. Living in SoCal helped."

"Wait, you lived in SoCal? In the late '90s? I always assumed you were much, ah – younger than that?"

"Young in spirit, Dawg, but that's just my physical body. My outward appearance, my soul, it's as old as you. But I digress. You're really busting up my flow here."

"I apologize."

"It's OK. There's a reason I'm Black Dog and you're just this dude who goes by different names depending on whether he's talking in the 1st, 2nd or 3rd person. But even that's inconsistent. Smacks of a disconnected, evil narcissism."

"Please, go on."

"He didn't start, but I had to watch, just to catch a glimpse. When he stepped on the court, it just *felt* like a happening. No matter what actually *happened.*"

"Fast forward to 1999 when I bought my 1st pair of basketball shoes since 1987 and they were Adidas because that's what Kobe wore, and I didn't care that he came up short against the Spurs because he came up short while still demanding the ball."

*"Wait... you bought basketball shoes?
Did you buy two pairs of the same
kind or different models for front and
back paws?"*

"Good question. If you'd done your
homework, you'd know I'm a
sneakerhead. Of course, I went with
two different styles. Both Adidas.
Again, though. My flow can't take
much more of this. Shall I continue?"

*"Yes. Please pardon my
impertinence."*

"ANYHOO. Finally, that summer of
1999, the Lakers brought in a coach
worthy of their talent. Phil Jackson.
Who but the Zen Master could get the
most out of the likes of Shaq and
Kobe? But Kobe was still the hot
sauce to Shaq's carne asada.
Irreplaceable and utterly necessary,
but it doesn't make the meal."

"And then, in 2004, the Pistons'
collection of no-names ended the
Shaq-Kobe Era. A Lakers team with
perhaps the greatest, weighted
average, collective roster resume in
NBA history – Shaq, Kobe, Gary

Payton, Karl Malone). But no chemistry = no rings. Life parallels abound."

"Shaq moved on, but Kobe stuck by our Lakers and gave us 12 more seasons and two more titles and an 81-POINT GAME. From Rookie Year Slam Dunk Champ to back-to-back Finals MVPs in the 4th quarter of his Picasso-like pro hoops career. It's not just Kobe's Lakers. It's Kobe's NBA. Then just like that it's 2016 and a 60-point final night and "Mamba Out" [watched on my phone the next day because I'm on the East Coast now and, you know, bedtime.] Bring on the HOF. MAD FLAVA INDEED. And then..."

"OK. This is just too much. YOU had a PHONE? And watched Kobe's final game on it? How'd you work the touch screen with those paws?"

"Listen, asshole, this is Black Dog you're talkin' at. Not some chump. Not a sucka. Dig this and dig it straight: MY PAWS WORKED THAT TOUCH SCREEN JUST FINE!"

"Got it. Go on, please."

"No. Call me back when you've learned the meaning of the word respect. I've got a fenceline to run and nice families to scare. Time to get my bark on."

"I brought you a bully stick..."

"Please, Ruprecht. You know I can't be bought."

"Fair enough. Favorite '90s rock artist?"

"Too easy. Let's do this Jeopardy-style. I'll answer in the form of a question: Who's still here?"

"Hmm... Staley... no. Cobain... no. Weiland... no. Cornell... no. Aww... c'mon Black Dog, gimme a break."

"Hey, hey, hey... one break... comin' up... BILLY FUCKING CORGAN, THAT'S WHO'S STILL HERE!"

"Black Dog, you CAN NOT be serious! The freaking Pumpkins?"

"One and the same, my brother.
Billy holds up. And holds weight.
Gravitas. Epic Pageantry. Pure
Drama. Check him out on Rogan.
2017. Best ever.

"I'll take your word for it."

HEAD SHAKER

black dog
delivers
 jaw-draped rope

i pull
he pulls
i stop
he shakes
i throw
he runs

black dog
never asks
why?

his rope never dies

YOU CAN'T

be The Shaman.
be The Brujo.

Not as manager, nor managed.

The Medicine Man can't be tamed.
He dies in captivity.
Wisdom bursts from freedom.
Of thought, word, action.

We seek those free
in ways
we aren't.
The ones who think
in ways
we can't.

Until we get beyond *hear*.
Until we *listen*.
Until we *dare*.

There and then
cracks begin.
Fissures in
your façade.
Windows to
the other side.

Now we exude humility.

Unable to walk another
or *another's* path.
Only our own, original – untrod.

Old tracks
cloud our thoughts.
Our way becomes clear.

RIGHTHERE MAN (cont.)

"You know, Ruprecht... you... err...
Black Dog isn't the only one with
something to say about Kobe. But
I'm gonna spare you my agony. For
now.

No, instead, listen (for once) to three
logline ideas for my latest
screenplay."

DRY HOLE

1) Raven-haired espionage
   enchantress stumbles upon a
   globalist death-cult's fiendish
   plan to steal a potentially
   planet-destroying McGuffin.

2) Black latex-clad sultry super
spy enlists her sorority sister-
turned bubble tea tycoon in a
daring rescue operation.

3) Ebony-tressed covert-ops
protégé flips the script on her
Machiavellian mentor just in
time to save a future President
from certain death at the
hands of a Mephistophelian
arch-criminal.

"That's great, Aung. Sounds like a
really nice piece of, uh... [sneer]
creative writing. It appears you cast
yourself as the star-lette? Or is that
just coincidence? Let me guess, all
the straight, white males are
complete buffoons... or... wait for it...
in this sure-to-be imbecilic Universe,
they're completely written out?"

"I knew you weren't paying
attention."

> *dogs freed*
> *from cages*
> *did leashes*
> *improve*
> *their lot?*

You continue critiquing:

"You've got a decent setup and satisfying finish – killing the greasy, white-privilege son of the military-industrial complex turned politician – but where's the inciting action?
The meat of the plot?
The twists?
The reversals of fortune?"

"All in my head, Ruprecht. Doth infereth too much from three prospective loglines."

"Powers of intuition far beyond your estimation. Always a strong "NT." Weaker on the "I" and "P." No fluke, either. I've taken that sucker least five times. Would you rather?"

"RUPRECHT !!! I'm asking for your help here. Do I need to spell it out? And, if I must spell it out, are YOU really the man to ask?"

"I doubt it. All I know for sure is never break Rule #1:"

avoid that which you don't like

"How's that apply here?"

After an appropriately pregnant, dramatic pause, you redirect:

"I have a proposition for you. Let's ditch our entirely suspect Turks and Caicos task, go on the lamb, and make this act pay."

"What act?"

"Our filled with S-T aimless banter. We land in 10. Then, it's customs chaos and right back into The Syndicate's maelstrom. Do you know how to sail?"

"I do. You taught me once, many years ago. Back then I went by *Aung*."

Your mind races. Seabiscuit on dianabol with bennies for breakfast...

TRÈS MAGNIFIQUE

not the most
coveted pattaya bargirl
not compared to
yen's visage
gi's derrière
rose's latina-with-
        chinese-eyes 'tude
all showier
than aung

with her quirky-for-the-kingdom
not-so-deferential personality
gymnast tight snare drum body
khmer-round strangeface
now she, she caught your eye
and you hers

though you never ventured to ask
from whence the scars, rendered
nigh invisible in the *Tahitian
Temptress'* black light glow – or was
it the original, *South Seas Siren*, just
down the block?

what mattered is you struck the right
notes in the dark and in the neon
lights on the street in the musky
night with scents of alley piss and
curry and saltwater and booze and 2-

stroke motorbike and jeepney
exhaust and of course back at your
poolside true toadman villa down
sattahip way and on your deliciously
lost weekend to *Ko Samui* where you
chartered a dhow,
sailing forth to *Ko Tao,*
ostensibly for the bouldering,
but knowing full well,
your five ten anasazi's
were securely kit-bagged back in
Coronado garage
A-HA!
tear up the planks and reveal,
                with dramatic effect,

The Syndicate's not-so hidden hand!

RIGHTHERE MAN (cont.)

"Good. Because I forgot. But I can
certainly turn cranks and navigate
for our crew of two. Jibe ho, matey!"

"Well, it's certainly nice to be part of
a professional organization."

"It'll be a ship most taut; I assure
you. Are you familiar with one
legendarily obscure, sparsely habited
Mar de Sur isle *O-Pitcairn's* ?"

EPILOGUE

daybreak's quiet retreat
blue-ish pink glow
ascends
birds renew
daily chatter
palm fronds
hold fast
to stillness
savoring final
windless moments
while seabreeze forces
its way onshore
rattling earth's cage
in protest
to silver king's reign
you threw the fly twice
because you [almost] never
do it right
the first time
but kings [the benevolent ones]
allow for second chances
[but rarely thirds]
and he knew you for a rube anyway
swallowing it
like he thought it was real
newsflash: he didn't
kings just like to make you
feel good about yourself
occasionally

playing God
but not seriously
the mark of true royalty
and now
whole sky buzzards
spinning, whirling
sunset ritual
35 knot westerlies
lit their fuse
pattern unrefined
yet not formless
look again
total chaos
stasis zero
our moment's passing
inevitable

Made in United States
Orlando, FL
04 July 2024

48613476R00093